谢志高画集

A COLLECTION OF PAINTINGS BY XIE ZHIGAO

北京美術攝影出版社

PUBLISHED BY BEIJING ARTS AND PHOTOGRAPHY PUBLISHING HOUSE

封面題字：吳作人
責任編輯：巴　莉
裝幀設計：
中華人民共和國印刷

Cover Inscription by Wu Zuoren
Editor in Charge:
Designer:　　Ba Li
PRINTED IN THE PEOPLE'S REPUBLIC
OF CHINA

謝 志 高 畫 集

北京美術攝影出版社　出版
（北京北三環中路六號）
新華書店北京發行所　發行
精美彩色印刷有限公司　製版印刷
12開本　6印張
1992年6月第1版第1次印刷
ISBN 7−80501−134−6/J·130

004000

谢志高

作者簡歷
Curriculum Vitae

謝志高、男，1942年6月生于上海。祖籍廣東省潮陽縣人。中國美術家協會會員、中國畫研究院專業畫家、副研究員。自幼喜畫，14歲即开始在報刊上發表美術作品。

1958年考入廣州美術學院附中。

1966年畢業于廣州美術學院中國畫系。

1968年到河北省工作，任美術編輯，辦《河北畫刊》。

1978年考取中央美術學院中國畫研究生。

1980年畢業，留中央美術學院中國畫系任教。

1987年底調入中國畫研究院，從事創作與研究。

1988年秋率團訪日，參加中日水墨畫展覽及交流活動。

1989年春應邀返故鄉汕頭市，舉辦個人畫展。

1990年春應邀赴香港，舉辦個人畫展。

1990年夏應邀赴泰國舉辦個人畫展。

1991年底——1992年，爲美國福布萊特基金會受聘學者，赴美講學。

作品曾多次參加國內外重大展覽，幷爲美術館、博物館、藝術院校、社會團體等收藏。幾十年來，發表、出版了許多中國畫、插圖、連環畫等作品。曾獲北京優秀美術作品獎，全國連環畫二等獎，國際水墨畫優秀獎等。主要論著有《工筆人物新畫》、《中國畫小輯》、《寫意人物畫技法》、《水墨仕女畫技法》、《謝志高畫集》等。

Xie Zhigao was born in Shanghai in June 1942. His parents came from Chaoyang County, Guangdong Province. He is a member of the Chinese Artists' Association, a professional painter and boundless spaces researcher at the Academy of Chinese Painting. He was zealously interested in painting in his childhood, and his works began to appear in newspapers and magazines when he was 14 years old.

1958—entered the middle school attached to the Guangzhou Academy of Fine Arts

1966—graduated from the Chinese Painting Department of the Guangzhou Academy of Fine Arts

1968—was fine arts editor for *Hebei Pictorial* in Hebei Province

1978—entered the Central Academy of Fine Arts as a graduate student of Chinese painting

1980—graduated from the Central Academy of Fine Arts and became a teacher in the Chinese Painting Department

End of 1987—entered the Academy of Chinese Painting to engage in artistic creation and research

Autumn of 1988—visited Japan as leader of a group to take part in the Sino-Japanese Ink-Wash Painting Exhibition and cultural exchange activities

Spring of 1989—invited to hold a one-man painting exhibition in Shantòu

Spring of 1990—invited to hold a one-man painting exhibition in Hong Kong

Summer of 1990—invited to hold a one-man painting exhibition in Thailand

The end of 1991——1992, invited as a scholar, by the Fulbright Foundation to give lectures in U.S.A.

His works have been displayed in many important exhibitions at bome and abroad and have been collected by galleries, museums, academies and universities of fine arts, and social groups. Over the years he has published many Chinese paintings, plates and picture stories. He has won the Beijing Excellent Artwork Award, second prize in the National Picture-Story Awards and an international prize for excellent ink-wash paintings. His works include *New Figure Paintings in "Gongbei" Style, Collection of Chinese Paintings, Techniques of Freehand Figure Painting, Ink-wash Techniques for Painting Ladies* and *Collection of Xie Zhigao's Paintings.*

剛柔相濟

——讀謝志高的人物畫

邵大箴

　　人物畫，尤其是現代人物畫，雖然在"五四"之後，已取得不少成果，涌現出徐悲鴻、蔣兆和、葉淺予、程十髮、 黃冑等名家，中青年畫家中也不乏創新者，但人們對人物畫仍然不滿足。部份原因是用水墨工具按西洋素描的辦法來畫人物，常常失去中國畫那種用線造型所形成的剛柔相濟的力感和韵味；而按傳統的一套來畫現代人物，舊瓶裝新酒，又不夠自然，且缺少現代美感。大體上說，"文革"前中國畫的工農兵人物主題畫，采用素描法的較多，這大概是導致八十年代的逆反心理和反復轉向文人小品畫的原因之一。文人小品畫，多畫古典人物，追求造型的變異、誇張和扭曲，雖有筆墨情趣，畢竟距離時代太遠，加上不少作者以"新文人"自居，競相追求畫風的放縱和飄逸，形成新的、令人憂慮的模式。在這種情況下，中國畫界的一些有識之士，心裡一直憋着一股氣，想在現代人物上做出成績來。中年畫家謝志高就是其中的一位。

　　謝志高受過嚴格的基礎訓練。他的寫實造型能力是很強的。青少年時代就在家鄉廣東嶄露頭角，後來長期生活在北方，邊做編輯邊從事繪畫創作。1978年考入中央美術學院國畫系研究生班，悉心鑽研。在蔣兆和、葉淺予等先生的直接指導和在中央美院特有的文化氛圍的薰陶下，思路更為开濶，藝術趨向成熟。他在熟練地掌握了西洋素描造型能力的情況下，進一步完善中國水墨傳統技法，特別注意領會和理解中國傳統人物畫的審美觀和造型觀，在用線、發揮水墨特性的傳神寫意上狠下功夫，使自己的作品更具內在力感和美。在美院執教及創作實踐中，均力倡現代人物畫，表現時代精神。他認為這方面的創作即使吃力不討好也應該堅持，因為這是時代的需要，也是文化和藝術積累的需要。當許多人從不同方面去嘗試，去努力、提供經驗，現代人物畫自然會形成規模，變劣勢為優勢，從而扭轉畫壇風氣。謝志高認為，現代人的生活是異常豐富、多樣的，給藝術家們的創造提供了極大的可能。

　　謝志高畫過有宏偉氣勢、造型語言如雕塑般的《建設者》，也畫過輕松活潑、猶如田園奏鳴曲的《曬穀》，還畫過以形象塑造見長的《凝思》、《祝福》。他有時也畫古代人物、如杜甫、李清照、蘇東坡等，那是藉助這些人物形象來抒發胸懷，寄托自己的感情，表現今人的思考。在近年的作品中，當推他最下功夫，也是畫界朋友們最為欣賞和贊揚的是他用了三四年時間搜集素材、反復醞釀琢磨和精心構思的水墨連環畫《春蠶》。他在充份發揮水墨特性的同時，成功地刻畫了茅盾這部宏篇巨制中的人物形象，性格塑造、環境描繪和氣氛渲染。既忠實于原著，又別有情趣。在四十幅不大的畫面上，幅幅都有畫家明確的立意和藝術追求。有人評價《春蠶》是水墨連環畫中的一塊碑石，是不過份的。在80年代中國畫壇的畫風越來越追求隨意和自由的情況下，這種認眞、嚴謹的精神和忠于現實主義創作原則的態度，尤其值得肯定。志高理解的現實主義是开放的，沒有絲毫保守和固步自封的味道。他深深懂得，只有借鑒一些藝術成果，古代的、現代的；中國的、外國的，幷消化它們，爲我所用，新的創造才會有深度，有力量。對這些，謝志高有深刻的思考。他是一位旣善于動手，又善于動腦、動心的畫家。他勤奮地學習藝術史和關注美術理論，幷參與研討。這，使他的作品具有某些理性的色彩。他又善于感受生活中千變萬化、新鮮活潑、觸動人們審美心靈的事物與現象，用生動的繪畫語言捕捉和描繪那些微妙的細節，這又使他的作品散發出濃郁的生活氣息。

　　還有一點特別使人稱道的，是謝志高兼具南方的靈秀之美和北方的豪邁氣勢。對此，他的好友、著名畫家林墉有過一段精彩的分析。他說，謝志高“從畫小艇流水到畫驢馬高粱，南北的跨越，着實懸殊。但謝志高克服了，駕御了，熟練了。就畫風而論，他以南方人的細膩飛動、清新明麗給厚苴的北國風光披上了輕紗，與沉重的嘆息迴異。他的畫奏出了北國笛音。而他筆下的南方圖畫，卻由于長期的北國風雪的蕩滌，都自然而然地揉進了一股蒼莽的陽剛，平添幾分硬朗的正氣。也許正因爲這一點，他的畫風在目前畫壇的南北殊異中迸出光彩，令人刮目相看。”

　　嚴格的寫實造型與水墨韵味的巧妙結合也好，理性思考的清晰力量與豐富感情有機交融也好，南方的輕松柔和與北方的粗獷厚樸諧和地集于一體也好，都說明謝志高的藝術兼有剛柔相濟的特色。我以爲，畫家風格成熟的標志是其創造的圖像語言連續性與獨一無二性的統一。連續性說明他有所承繼、有所延續；獨一無二性，說明他的創造和發揮。沒有連續性的獨一無二性，容易把藝術創造引向過份的荒誕、而失去“控制”。缺少獨一無二性的連續性，又幾乎是創造性品格的喪失，于藝術發展無益。謝志高的人物畫是有傳統精神的，又是有個性的。他從衆多的人物畫家中“跳”了出來——以其剛柔相濟的圖像語言。他現在正值創作旺盛期，他在勤奮地實踐，似乎在強化自己這種剛柔相濟的形象。

　　已經在好手如林的中國畫壇上爭得一席位置的謝志高，還會有更光輝的前程，因爲剛柔相濟的創造，能夠提供無限的可能，使他的智慧、才能、膽識和靈性得到充份的發揮。

一九九一年二月十二日于帥府園寓所煮墨齋

Boldness and Gentleness Combined

--Xie Zhigao's Figure Paintings

Shao Dazhen

Although figure painting, particularly modern figure painting, progressed remarkably after the May Fourth New Cultural Movement in 1919 and, besides master painters like Xu Beihong, Jiang Zhaohe, Ye Qianyu, Cheng Shifa and Huang Zhou, younger painters tried their hands at new techniques too. Their works were far from satisfactory, partly because figures drawn with Western techniques using Chinese ink and brushes lost the impact and appeal of the bold but gentle effect created by the lines used in traditional Chinese painting. Yet, a modern figure done with traditional methods seemed unnatural and lacking in modernity, like putting new wine into an old bottle. Generally speaking, before the "cultural revolution" Chinese figure painting concentrated on sketching workers, peasants and soldiers. It was probable that the circumstance led to the antagonistic mentality and the reversal changes in the 1980s, when artists turned away from it to small literati painting instead.

Small literati painting depicted ancient figures with variation, exaggeration and distortion. Although exquisitely executed, they were far removed from modern life. Also, many painters who called themselves the "new literati" adopted an upsetting indulgent style in their work. Under such circumstances some Chinese painters, including the middle-aged Xie Zhigao, sought to create a new, modern figure painting.

Xie Zhigao had strict training and is good at realistic portrayal. In his teens he became known as a painter in Guangdong, his home province. Afterward, he moved north to Hebei and worked as a fine arts editor and continued to paint. In 1978 he entered the graduate class of the Chinese Traditional Painting Department of the Central Academy of Fine Arts for further training. Under the direct guidance of famous painters such as Jiang Zhaohe and Ye Qianyu, and owing to the special cultural atmosphere of the Academy, his vision broadened and he matured artistically. Having mastered Western painting techniques, he tried to perfect the traditional techniques of Chinese ink-wash painting by paying special attention to the concepts of aesthetics and form of traditional figure painting, making special effort in the use of lines and bringing out the characteristics of ink-and-wash and the freehand style. All these gave his works inner power and beauty.

While teaching in the Academy he advocated modern figure painting which reflects the spirit of the era, insisting that the times, culture and art demanded it, even though the creation of such work was painstaking and unappreciated. If artists exerted themselves and made contribution with their exploration, modern figure painting would naturally take shape and prevail, and the opinion of painting circles would be altered. Xie also thought that the rich colorful life of modern people offered great possibilities for artists.

Xie Zhigao's **Builders** has the grandeur of a sculpture, his **Drying Grains** is lively as a pastural sonata, his **Thinking** and **Blessing** portray distinctive characters. He paints ancient figures too: such as Du Fu (712—770), a famous Tang Dynasty poet, Li Qingzhao (1084-1151), a famous woman poet of the Southern Song Dynasty, and Su Dongpo (1037-1101), a famous Northern Song Dynasty poet. He painted them in order to express his thoughts and emotions. He spent years in collecting material before **Spring Silkworm** took shape in his mind. When it was painstakingly done, it was most appreciated and won praises from his artist friends. It was a serial ink-wash painting portraying the characters in the novel **Spring Silkworm** (by the famous

Chinese writer Mao Dun) and the environment and atmosphere they lived in. The picture story is not only faithful to the original, but also attractive. Each of the forty paintings has a clear approach and artistic pursuit. It is no exaggeration to call the picture story a monument of ink-wash picture stories. While many painters were doing what they pleased with traditional Chinese paintings in the 1980s, his conscientious and rigorous attitude and realistic approach were particularly praiseworthy.

Realism, in Xie's opinion, is open to progress and free from conservatism or restriction. He realized that only by studying and digesting all artistic achievement, both ancient and modern, domestic and foreign, making it his own, would one's new creations be profound and powerful. Xie believes a painter must use his hand, mind and heart. He studies art history and theories of fine art and often takes part in discussions. These add theory to his work. He is also susceptible to changeable phenomena that are new and lively and are able to awaken people's aesthetic sense. He catches and describes these subtle details in vivid artistic language, imbuing his paintings with a strong dash of everyday life.

Xie Zhigao has both the gentle cleverness of a southerner and the bold generosity of a northerner. Lin Yong, a famous painter and one of his best friends, once said, "It is a wonder that Xie Zhigao paints both small boats and streams of the south and donkeys, horses and sorghum of the north. He not only bridges the gap, but is well-versed in them. As for style, he drapes light gauzes over northern scenery in the southerner's subtle way which is redolent with beauty and freshness. Instead of a heavy sigh, his paintings bring out the music of a north China flute. At the same time, his living for long periods in the north gives his sceneries of the south a tinge of masculinity and uprightness. Perhaps just because of this, his paintings radiate light and color, and stand out between the two different styles."

The exquisite combination of realistic form and ink-wash charm, the mixture of reason and emotion, the harmonious integration of the elegant gentleness of the south and the straightforward honesty of the north all contribute to the merging of boldness and gentleness in Xie Zhigao's paintings. A painter's maturity is marked by the consistency and uniqueness of his artistic language. Consistency shows that the painter has inherited and carries on the heritage; uniqueness shows his creativity and elaboration. Uniqueness without consistency will easily lead to absurdity, and art would be "out of control"; consistency without uniqueness will lead to the loss of creativity, which is harmful for the development of art. Xie Zhigao's figure paintings contain both tradition and personality. He stands out among so many other figure painters through his own artistic language combining boldness with gentleness. Now at the apex of his creation he is still trying to strengthen this characteristics of his.

Xie Zhigao, who has found his place in Chinese painting among a large number of outstanding painters, has an even brighter future, because the combination of boldness and gentleness provides countless opportunities for him to give full play to his wisdom, ability, courage, insight and intelligence.

Zhumo Studio   Shuaifuyuan Residence

February 12, 1991

沙田綠雨　(136×68cm)
The Rain Fallen upon the Green Environment

春之夢　(68×68cm)

Spring Dream

倦繡圖　(68×68cm)

Pausing Between A Long
Embroidering

建設者　(102×97cm)
Builders

一江春水　(68×68cm)
The Spring View of the River

春日　　(68×68cm)

A Spring Day

竹樓小憩　(46×34cm)

**Taking A Rest in A
Bamboo Building**

版納即景　(46×34cm)

A Scene of Xishuangbanna

曬 穀 (68×68cm)

Drying Grains

藏　婦 (68×45cm)

A Tibetan Woman

老把式　(135×135cm)

A Veteran Driver

暮 色　(47×47cm)

The Dusk

春雨濛濛　(68×68cm)

Drizzling Spring Rain

李清照詞意　(90×68cm)

**According to A Ci-poem
by Li Qingzhao**

将相和 (82×44cm)
**Reconciliation between
the Minister and General**

屈子求索　(68×68cm)
Qu Yuan

伯樂相馬 (68×68cm)
Bo Le Judging A Horses

霸王别姬　(68×68cm)
Ba Wang Bidding Yu Ji Farewell

鐘馗嫁妹　(68×68cm)
**Zhong Kui Sending His
Sister to Marriage**

東坡覓石　(68×68cm)
Su Dongpo Looking
for Stones

杜甫行吟　(68×45cm)

Du Fu Reciting A Poem on A Trip

東坡醉吟　(68×68cm)

Intoxicated Su Dongpo
Composing Poetry

黛玉葬花 (68×68cm)

Lin Daiyu Burying
Flowers

仕 女 (68×45cm)
The Beauty

世人騎大馬 我擱
只不然一跨子
跨馿子回頭擔
王梵志詩意
柴漢 七扇大廣年北京張
[印章]

王梵志詩意　(68×68cm)
According to A Poem by Wang Fanzhi

東坡采荔　(68×68cm)
Su Dongpo Gathering Lichi

吟春圖　(68×45cm)

**Reciting A Poem about
the Spring Scenery**

王維詩意　(68×68cm)
According to A Poem
by Wang Wei

滄浪亭詩意　(68×68cm)

According to A Poem about the Cang Lang Pavilion

國破山河在，城春草木深。感時花濺淚，恨別鳥驚心。烽火連三月，家書抵萬金。白頭搔更短，渾欲不勝簪。

杜甫春望詩意 志高寫於北京喘吟齋

春望詩意　(68×68cm)
According to A Poem by Du Fu

鐘馗聽風圖　(136×68cm)
Zhong Kui Listening to
the Soughing Wind

東坡賞硯　(68×68cm)
Su Dongpo Appreciating
Ink-slabs

東籬把酒黃昏後　(68×68cm)
After Drinking

夢 荷 (68×68cm)
Dreaming of Lotus

春　雨　(135×135cm)
Spring Rain

凝 思 (84×68cm)

Being Lost in Thought

好朋友 (68×45cm)

Good Friends

水鄉姑娘　(68×46cm)
Girl in the Region
of Rivers and Lakes

沙田姑娘　(47×35cm)
Girl in Shatian

中學生　　　(47×35cm)
Middle School Student

漁 民 (34×28cm)
Fisher

船老大 (34×28cm)
The Boatman

山東漢子　(34×28cm)
Shandong Man

山邨大娘　(34×28cm)
Aunty of the Mountain Village

農民本色　(68×45cm)
Showing the True Quality of A Peasant

海港一兵 （68×45cm）

A Worker of the Port

黄河頌　(180×180cm)

Ode to the Yellow River

黄河颂局部
**Ode to the Yellow
River (Detail)**

鄉村喜事 (180×180cm)
Joyous Occasion in the
Mountain Village

鄉村喜事 局部
Joyous Occasion
in the Mountain
Village (Detail)

鄉村喜事 局部
Joyous Occasion
in the Mountain
Village (Detail)

《春蠶》之7(47×35cm)

No.7 of Spring Silkworm

《春蠶》之11(47×35cm)

No.11 of Spring Silkworm

《春蠶》之12(47×35cm)
No.12 of Spring Silkworm

《春蠶》之16(47×35cm)

No.16 of Spring Silkworm

《春蠶》之21(47×35cm)

No.21 of Spring Silkworm

《春蠶》之22(47×35cm)
**No.22 of Spring
Silkworm**

《春蠶》之24(47×35cm)

**No.24 of Spring
Silkworm**

《春蠶》之33(47×35cm)

No.33 of Spring

Silkworm

《春蠶》之34(47×35cm)

**No.34 of Spring
Silkworm**

《春蠶》之38(47×35cm)
No.38 of Spring Silkworm

《春蠶》之39(47×35cm)

No.39 of Spring Silkworm